KIDNAPPED

From its first moments right through to an ending full of surprises, Kidnapped *moves at a very fast pace. It is one of the greatest adventure stories of all time.*

LADYBIRD BOOKS, INC.
Auburn, Maine 04210 U.S.A.
© LADYBIRD BOOKS LTD 1989
Loughborough, Leicestershire, England

Printed in England

KIDNAPPED

by Robert Louis Stevenson

retold by John Grant
illustrated by Terry Gabbey

Ladybird Books

My troubles began the moment that I knocked on the iron-studded door of the House of Shaws. There I stood, David Balfour, in the warmth of a June evening. I was seventeen, and my parents were dead. I had a few shillings in my pocket. I also had a letter of introduction to my uncle, Ebenezer Balfour of Shaws. He was my only relative, and a rich man.

A sound made me look up... into the muzzle of a musket. From an open window a voice called, "Who's there?" My uncle had welcomed me to the House of Shaws.

Grudgingly, Uncle Ebenezer gave me a
meal and a bed for the night. The house
was a grim barracks of a building, partly
unfinished. Even those parts that *were*
complete were damp and crumbling. I had
thought that the Laird of Shaws would live
in style. My uncle lived alone, a miser, hated
by all the people in the countryside around.

The night after I arrived, the weather grew stormy. As we sat by a feeble fire in the kitchen, Uncle Ebenezer handed me a key. "Fetch me down the chest from the room at the top of the tower," he said.

The tower entrance was outside the house, and I groped my way in the glare of the lightning. Halfway to the top, a brighter flash than before filled the tower with light... and I saw that I stood on the edge of the last complete step. Below me was a dark, yawning gap. Another inch and I would have fallen to my death.

Afraid and angry, I returned to the kitchen. Uncle Ebenezer looked up, startled, as I entered. Then he fell to the floor in a faint. Had he planned to murder me?

The next morning, my uncle treated my near-disaster as a joke. He had business in the nearby town of Queensferry, he said, and invited me to accompany him. The business was with his lawyer, Rankeillor, and a Captain Hoseason of the brig *Covenant*.

We met the captain at an inn, and I started a conversation with the ship's boy. He told me that the *Covenant* regularly carried convicted criminals and other unwilling passengers to become slaves in the American colonies.

When the captain invited us to visit his ship where it lay at anchor, I was eager to go. My uncle and I were rowed out to the vessel. I was first aboard. I turned in time to see the boat and Uncle Ebenezer heading back toward the shore. Then a heavy blow to the head sent me tumbling, senseless, on the deck.

I awoke to find myself a prisoner below decks, where I remained for many days while the ship sailed north, then west between the islands of Orkney and Shetland. Then I was allowed on deck, only to find that the wind had turned foul and was pushing us steadily south.

To make matters worse, the weather grew foggy. As the sailors peered into the murk, there was a cry, then a crash. The *Covenant* had collided with another vessel. It was a

fishing boat, and quickly lost to view, but not before one man had leaped up, grabbed hold of the *Covenant*'s bowsprit, and pulled himself to safety.

That is how I came to meet Alan Breck Stewart. He was a short man, and something of a dandy in his plumed hat, blue coat with silver buttons, and sword by his side.

I had been put to work in the roundhouse,
a cabin in the middle part of the ship which
doubled as officers' quarters and ship's
armory. Alan was quartered in the roundhouse,
and I quickly got to know him. We had
something in common—neither of us was a
willing passenger. As we became friends, I
learned that he was a Jacobite. When Prince
Charlie failed to win the throne in 1746, his
followers fled, many abroad. Alan Breck
Stewart was one of these. But during the last
five years he had returned to Scotland many
times in secret, to collect money for Ardshiel,
his exiled clan chief. He was completing such
a mission when his boat was run down by the
Covenant. He carried the money, a fortune in
gold coins, in a belt around his waist.

But the captain and crew found out about the belt of gold, and were determined to have it. We barricaded ourselves in the roundhouse. I loaded all the pistols I could find, while Alan, sword drawn, stationed himself by the door. And not a moment too soon. Led by the captain, the crew stormed the roundhouse. The battle was fast and furious. Twice we repelled attack, partly by my firing pistols out the window, but chiefly by Alan's brilliant swordsmanship.

"Am I not a great fighter?" he cried in triumph. Then he rewarded me for my part in the victory with a silver button cut from his coat.

With most of the crew dead or wounded, the captain asked for a truce. Alan made him agree to land him on the shore of Loch Linnhe, close to his own clan country of Appin. But the ship, shorthanded now, was difficult to manage. In the middle of the night she ran onto a reef off the coast of the island of Mull. Stuck fast, she was helpless in the path of a giant wave. In a moment I was swept overboard. Clinging to a spar, I was carried ashore by the current onto a small, barren island.

For four days I wandered the island, exhausted, cold, and hungry. I ate raw shellfish, and wept with frustration at the closeness of the main island across a narrow strait. To make it worse, I could see the smoke from a chimney rising above a low hill. Then the crew of a fishing boat hailed me and pointed to the strait. And I realized that when the tide was at its lowest ebb the channel between the islands almost dried out. Not wasting another moment, I waded across, the water little more than knee-deep. By evening, I reached the house whose chimney smoke I had seen.

It was a small cottage, built of stone, with a turf roof. An old man sat at the door smoking his pipe. He told me that the survivors of the wreck of the *Covenant* had already passed that way. Then I showed him Alan's silver button. "Ah," he said, "I have a message for the lad with the button. You are to go by way of Torosay to join your friend in Appin."

After a meal and a night's rest, I said good-by to the old gentleman and his wife. Four days of walking took me across Mull to Torosay. From there I crossed by ferry to Lochaline on the mainland. The ferry skipper was named Neil Roy Macrob. Alan had told me that the Macrobs were kin to the Appin Stewarts, and I again produced my button. And again there was a message for me.

I was to make my way to the house of John of the Claymore in Ardgour, and from there to seek out James of the Glens in Appin at a place called Aucharn. As I left the ferry, Neil Roy Macrob warned me to stay clear of patrols of the "red soldiers."

The inn at Lochaline was a miserable place. During the night it rained, and soon the water was ankle-deep. I was more than glad to leave early in the morning.

I was scarcely on my way when I caught up with a stout little man. He had a very solemn expression, read a book while he walked, and looked like a minister. He proved a pleasant (and useful) companion. He was a traveling preacher, and a Lowlander like myself. His name was Henderland. He told me about the troubles that had befallen the Highlands after the defeat of the Jacobites. When he spoke of the ''Red Fox,'' I grew suddenly alert. On board ship Alan had mentioned that name often, usually in anger. He had even sworn to kill the man known as the Red Fox. Who was he? I asked.

The Red Fox, explained Mr. Henderland, was the nickname of Colin Campbell of Glenure. He was one of the king's agents sent to administer the lands of dead or exiled Jacobites. Everyone in Appin hated him and would have dearly loved to see him dead.

I spent that night as a guest of Mr. Henderland.

The next morning, Mr. Henderland arranged
for me to be taken across Loch Linnhe in a
fishing boat. As the boat neared the shore,
I saw a column of the "red soldiers"
marching by the lochside into Appin. The
fishermen put me ashore where the Wood of
Lettermore came close to the water's edge.
The trees clung to the steep mountainside,
and a narrow, twisting track served as a road.
I was sitting by a spring eating the oat bread
Mr. Henderland had given me for my journey
when I heard the sound of men and horses.

Leading their mounts along the track came
four men. One was obviously a Highland
servant, with a leather traveling bag and a
sack of lemons slung on his horse's back. In
front of him was a man whose black clothes
and white wig showed that he was a
lawyer. Bringing up the rear was a man in
the uniform of a Sheriff's Officer.

But it was the leader of the party who
caught my special attention. He was a bluff,
red-headed figure of commanding
appearance who fanned himself with his hat
in the noonday heat.

I rose and asked the way to Aucharn.

"Whom do you seek in Aucharn?" asked the red-headed man.

"James of the Glens," I replied.

At this the travelers looked closely at me and spoke among themselves. As the lawyer addressed the big man, I realized that I was face to face with Colin Campbell of Glenure — the Red Fox.

He turned to speak to me again. He had barely uttered more than a few words when the sound of a shot echoed through the trees and he fell dead on the road.

I turned and scrambled up the mountainside. In an open glade I glimpsed a tall man wearing a black coat and carrying a long gun.

"The murderer!" I cried. "I see him!"

I looked back down to the road. A party of redcoats had appeared and, muskets in hand, were already climbing through the trees toward me. I waved at them to hurry, but as I did so I heard the lawyer shout, "Ten pounds if you take that lad! He's an accomplice, posted here to hold us in talk!"

I stood rooted to the spot. Then a voice said, "Quick! In here among the trees!" As I dived for cover, bullets were already cracking through the branches, and I found myself face to face with Alan Breck Stewart.

"Come!" he said, and I followed at a run along the mountainside. Through birch scrub and over bare hillside we ran. We stooped for cover. We crawled swiftly in the heather. From time to time, Alan stood up so the soldiers could see him, and they shouted and came even faster in pursuit. I felt I could go no further, but Alan clapped me on the shoulder and I followed him as we climbed higher up the mountain. There was no revealing himself to the soldiers this time.

Finally we stopped, almost at the same place we had started from. I collapsed like a dead man. But our pursuers were already far away in the opposite direction.

I was troubled by the thought of Alan as an assassin. But he swore that another man had struck down the Red Fox, and our efforts had been to allow him to escape from the redcoat patrol.

As night fell we set off for Aucharn and James of the Glens. It was about half-past ten when we arrived. Lights streamed from every door and window. In the glare of torches, we saw men taking hidden weapons from under the thatch and hurrying off into the darkness to conceal them in a different place. As head of the Appin Stewarts in the absence of the chief, Ardshiel, James had to organize the hunt for the Red Fox's murderer. Alan and I were suspects, and "Wanted" notices would soon be out for us. Weapons were forbidden in the Highlands, and a search for wanted men might turn up much more. James quickly provided us with a change of clothes, a sword for me, some food, and a little money.

Then off we fled into the night, leaving James and his people to deal with the illegal weapons.

We went eastward. The country was wild
and sparsely inhabited. Alan stopped several
times to leave news of the murder at lonely
houses. And in our haste he misjudged the
way. By morning, instead of being safely
hidden, we found ourselves crossing the
floor of a vast, rock-strewn valley. High
mountains rose on each side. I know now
that we were in the wilderness called
Glencoe. The land was void of people, but
Alan pushed on. With difficulty we crossed
a foaming, rocky river.

As full daylight came upon the glen we
found a makeshift hiding place in a shallow

hollow where the tops of two huge boulders
leaned toward each other. Twenty feet
above the ground we were safe from
redcoat eyes on the valley floor. We prayed
that there would be no watchers on the
surrounding mountains.

Throughout that long, blazing summer day we lay on the burning rock. Shortly after daylight the soldiers arrived. They made camp half a mile away, and sentries took up positions on the open ground and on rocks almost as tall as our own. Far up the glen we saw horse soldiers moving back and forth through the heather. We had no water and were tortured with thirst. At one point we lay hardly daring to breathe as a sentry took his post directly below us.

At last the sun began to go down. Alan judged that it was safe to descend, and in the cover of the lengthening shadows and the scattered rocks we crept swiftly and cautiously along the valley floor. At dusk we reached a stream where we drank deeply and ate some food. Then we hurried on, striking upward to the mountains and away from the deadly valley of Glencoe.

High on the side of a mountain we came to a small wooded glen where trout swam in a stream and a cave promised shelter. Alan called it the Heugh of Corrynakiegh. Here we rested for several days.

But we could not stay there forever. One night Alan slipped away down the mountain and left word of our whereabouts with one

of his clansmen. Above all, we needed
money if Alan was to reach safety in France.
Three days later there came a reply. The
country was being combed by the redcoats.
James of the Glens had been arrested on
suspicion. And a reward of one hundred
pounds was offered for the capture of Alan
and me.

The messenger brought not only money
but one of the "Wanted" notices. I was
very badly described, and unlikely to be
recognized. But Alan was already too well
known for safety, and for a moment I was
tempted to strike off on my own for the
Lowlands and my own people.

The following morning we were on our way again. We came down from the mountains and onto a desolate moor. There was scarcely any cover, and we were forced to creep from bush to bush, easily visible to any watcher on the surrounding hills. The weather was still hot and cloudless, and our water bottle was soon empty.

At noon we rested. Alan took first watch. Then he slept while I sat guard. But I was tired and I soon fell asleep.

I woke with a start—almost too late. Mounted soldiers were approaching from the southeast. As I watched, they fanned out into an extended line covering about half a mile. Then they began a steady advance, probing the heather with their swords.

There was no way we could avoid being taken if we stayed. And if we fled before them, they would ride us down in minutes.

Alan woke and summed up the situation. "We must get clear of their line of advance. That mountain to the northeast is Ben Alder. It is a wild, deserted mountain full of hills and hollows, and if we can get to it before the moon rises, we may be all right."

Already exhausted, we once more fled for our lives. On our hands and knees much of the time, we worked our way across the half-mile of advancing cavalry. Even when evening fell and the soldiers were recalled for the night, we did not stop. The air grew cooler, and a heavy dew refreshed us.

But dawn found us numb with exhaustion, still blundering on. Too tired to keep a proper watch, we walked like blind men straight into an ambush.

Three or four wild Highlanders leaped from the heather and pinned us to the ground, their daggers at our throats. Then Alan said something in Gaelic, and immediately we were released. Together we headed for Ben Alder. I had the aid of two Highlanders, who took an arm each and carried me along as if I were a feather.

The lower part of the mountain was thickly wooded. The crags rose sheer above the trees. We found our place of refuge as guests of Cluny Macpherson, chief of Clan Vourich.

Instead of fleeing like other Jacobite chiefs, Cluny had remained in his own country. He had a number of hiding places, and now we were ushered into the one known as Cluny's Cage.

Where the trees grew out at an angle from the rock face, trunks and stout branches had been lashed between them to form a framework. Earth carried up the mountain made a level floor, and the whole structure was thatched and covered with moss to form a house that comfortably accommodated five or six people.

Alan introduced me to the chief as
Mr. David Balfour, Laird of Shaws, and we
sat down to a hot meal. This extraordinary
house, which looked for all the world like a
wasps' nest clinging to the mountain, even
had a fireplace. It was formed in a shallow
cave, the smoke going unnoticed against the
gray rock face above.

But even as I sat down to eat, the world
spun before my eyes. Terror, exhaustion,
and near starvation were having their effect.
Cluny's servants put me to bed, and I
remained there, only half conscious, for the
better part of three days. One of the
Highlanders, the chief's barber, was actually
a doctor by profession. I was put in his care
while Alan, whose toughness had enabled
him to recover by the end of the meal, spent
the time playing cards.

On the morning of the third day I felt well enough to get up. I went to the entrance of the Cage. The air felt fresh, and I was eager to be on my way. But Alan seemed worried and somewhat shamefaced. He confessed that in three days of card playing he had lost what little money we had.

Cluny generously offered to return his winnings, and I was glad to accept. But Alan's pride was hurt, and it was in gloomy silence that we left Cluny's Cage and set off down the mountain.

Our flight from the mounted soldiers had carried us many miles out of our way. Cluny provided us with a guide who led us first to Loch Ericht, which we crossed by night. He found us a hiding place on the shore of Loch Rannoch and gave us directions for the remainder of our journey to the Lowlands.

Alan was still sulking, and became furious when he realized that the route would not only take us from one mountaintop to another but also through Campbell country. He calmed down a little when Cluny's man explained that it was the last place anyone would expect to find two suspects in a Campbell murder hunt.

We soon lost the benefit of our rest in Cluny's Cage. The brilliant summer weather

gave way to cold, wind, and rain. Through
mist and low cloud we trudged, traveling by
night and sleeping on the sodden earth by
day. We both grew bad-tempered, and we
argued as we walked. Finally, we had a
furious quarrel over Alan's gambling with
our precious funds. In my anger I drew my
sword on Alan. That brought us to our
senses, and we were friends once more.

But our friendship did not make our suffering any the less. I was chilled to the bone and ached in every limb. I felt I would die if we did not find warmth and shelter soon. Finally, I could go no further. Alan thought we must be close to the Braes of Balquhidder. This was not the territory of one clan. The people of Balquhidder bore many names. Some were fugitives. There were several Macgregors, kin to the famous outlaw Rob Roy. There were also some Maclarens, who owed allegiance to the chief of Alan's people, the Appin Stewarts.

With one last effort I followed Alan down the bank of a raging stream till we came to a house. The people there were Maclarens. We had found yet another refuge.

Alan left me and went to find a hiding place for himself, but during the weeks when I was ill he visited me every evening. The news of our presence in Balquhidder spread quickly among the people of the Braes. I was attended by the local doctor, and my visitors were many. From where I lay,

I could see one of the "Wanted" posters on the wall. It was a strange life for a hunted man.

My host, Duncan Dhu Maclaren, played the bagpipes. Once I had regained some of my strength he would bring out his pipes in the evening, and often the music and laughter went on far into the night.

Not a single person made a move to betray us—even though there was a reward of a hundred pounds, and even though redcoat patrols were active in the region. I watched from my bed one day as a strong foot patrol and a party of mounted men went by. But they paid no heed to the scattered houses along the Braes.

One day a new visitor came to the Maclarens. He was Robin Oig Macgregor, son of Rob Roy. He and Alan were old rivals, and Duncan Dhu suggested that they settle

their differences with the pipes. Robin was
known as a fine musician, and so, to my
surprise, was Alan. Mrs. Maclaren set out
food and drink while Alan and Robin sat
themselves on either side of the fire. They
took turns playing, and *how* they played!
Never had music thrilled me so before. It
was close to morning when Alan had to
admit that Robin was the better of the two.

Like us, Robin Oig Macgregor was a
fugitive, but a less fortunate one. Less than
three years later he was caught and hanged.

Late in the summer I was considered well enough to travel. One last great barrier remained, the River Forth. The main bridge was at Stirling, close to the castle and its garrison of redcoats.

Alan thought that it was so long since the Appin murder that the hunt for us would have slackened. In that case, our best plan would be to take the most direct route to the Lowlands, by way of Stirling.

We left Balquhidder at night, and two days later came down out of the high hills and into the lowlands of the Carse of Stirling. The weather was warm, and we made camp on a small island where a tributary flowed into the Forth.

All day we lay hidden, eating and drinking and listening to the sound of harvesters in the fields along the river. Not far off we could see Stirling Castle. And nearby, below the castle, was the bridge, a narrow, steeply rising stone structure.

We set off downriver before the moon rose. There were lights in the castle and in the town, but everything was quiet. As Alan had hoped, there appeared to be no guard on the bridge.

We crept as close as we dared, and could still see no sentry. But we could not see over the crown of the arch, and decided to wait.

As we crouched in the shadow of a roadside ditch, we heard footsteps. An old woman was coming along the road. We heard her pass onto the bridge. The footsteps grew fainter. She was surely across by now. Then we heard a challenge—"WHO GOES?" —and the rattle of a musket. The bridge was indeed guarded.

What were we to do now? We had three shillings left. And between us and safety flowed a wide, swift river. Upstream the smaller bridges would also be guarded. So downstream we went, down toward where the river opened out into the Firth of Forth and the sea.

All night we followed the shore, avoiding towns and villages. Dawn found us near the hamlet of Limekilns. On the opposite shore I could see Queensferry, where my adventures had started many weeks earlier. Mr. Rankeillor the lawyer was there. He was the one hope I had of clearing my name, and of getting Alan safely to France. But between us and Queensferry there was a wide stretch of water, with ships at anchor and boats going to and fro.

That's what we needed—a boat.

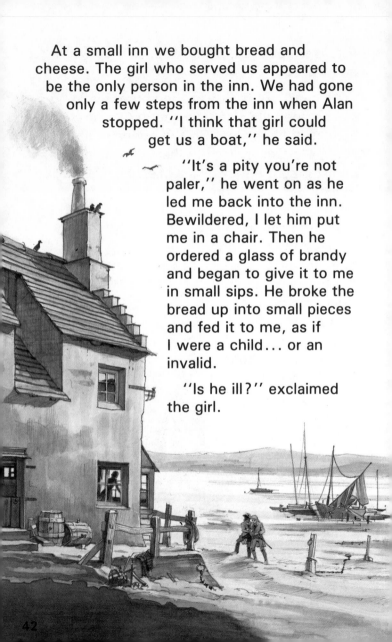

At a small inn we bought bread and cheese. The girl who served us appeared to be the only person in the inn. We had gone only a few steps from the inn when Alan stopped. "I think that girl could get us a boat," he said.

"It's a pity you're not paler," he went on as he led me back into the inn. Bewildered, I let him put me in a chair. Then he ordered a glass of brandy and began to give it to me in small sips. He broke the bread up into small pieces and fed it to me, as if I were a child... or an invalid.

"Is he ill?" exclaimed the girl.

"Ill?" cried Alan. "He has walked
hundreds of miles and slept in wet heather."

"Has he no friends?"

"Aye, he has," said Alan. "But without a
boat he cannot reach them. And what's
more..." Here, Alan leaned forward and
whistled softly a few notes. It was "Charlie
Is My Darling," a Jacobite song.

The girl gasped. "Is he...?"

"Indeed," said Alan. "And with a price
upon his head."

With that, the girl brought a hot meal, refusing payment. I asked her if she knew of Mr. Rankeillor the lawyer in Queensferry. Not only did she know of him, but she had heard very highly of him. More important, she was sure she could get us a boat.

We hid for the rest of the day in the woods close to the beach. Night fell, and the lights in the houses had long since gone out, when we heard the sound of oars. It was the girl from the inn. Not daring to trust anyone else, she had taken a neighbor's boat. She was a sturdy girl, and before long we stood on the Lothian shore.

We thanked her and bid her good night, and
watched until she vanished in the darkness on
her way back to Limekilns. I prayed that her
exploit would go undiscovered. The penalties
for helping wanted criminals were harsh.

In the light of day I made my way toward the town while Alan remained hidden in the fields. I walked along the main street of Queensferry, ragged and filthy. The well-clad, elegant-looking townspeople gave me strange looks. I even felt ashamed to stop someone and ask for Mr. Rankeillor. At last I stopped to rest by a handsome house on the landward side of the town. A finely dressed gentleman came down the steps. Plucking up my courage, I asked for the house of Mr. Rankeillor.

"This is it," he said. "And I am he."

From that moment everything changed. I told him that I was David Balfour. He took me into the house and had me tell my whole story. As a lawyer, he would have nothing to do with anything illegal. To protect himself, and others, he had me use false names. Cluny Macpherson became "Mr. Jameson" and Alan was called "Thomson."

I now discovered why my uncle had had me kidnapped. It seemed that Uncle Ebenezer was the younger son of the Balfours of Shaws. When my grandfather died, Ebenezer stayed in the House of Shaws to manage the estate. His elder brother, my father, went off to become schoolmaster of a remote village. On his death it was I, not Uncle Ebenezer, who was rightful Laird of Shaws. I was a rich man, with land and with money in the bank.

But what was I to do about Alan? Even if he were innocent of the murder of the Red Fox, he was still a wanted man as a Jacobite, among other things. But I could not abandon him now. It was Mr. Rankeillor who worked out a plan. But first we had to deal with Uncle Ebenezer.

Washed, fed, and dressed in clothes belonging to the lawyer's son, I set off with him and his clerk as night fell. I took them to where Alan lay hidden and explained the plan. Then we walked on toward the House of Shaws.

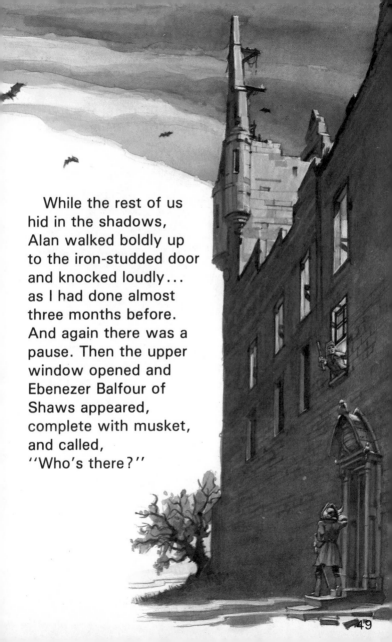

While the rest of us
hid in the shadows,
Alan walked boldly up
to the iron-studded door
and knocked loudly...
as I had done almost
three months before.
And again there was a
pause. Then the upper
window opened and
Ebenezer Balfour of
Shaws appeared,
complete with musket,
and called,
"Who's there?"

49

Alan persuaded him that he had urgent business and that he had better come down and open the door. Uncle Ebenezer did so. Sitting on the top step and pointing the gun at Alan, he said, "What's your business, then?"

Alan said that he was a partner of Captain Hoseason. Since the ship had been wrecked off Mull, David Balfour could not be sold as a slave in America. He was being held captive to be ransomed...or killed. Which did Ebenezer prefer? Confused, Ebenezer blundered from one lie to another, until he realized that he had been tricked into a confession: he had paid Hoseason to kidnap me and sell me as a slave in the Carolinas.

At that, we stepped from the shadows.

"Good evening, Mr. Balfour," said the lawyer.

"Good evening, Uncle," said I.

Uncle Ebenezer said not a word.

Still speechless, he let Mr. Rankeillor lead him into the house. We followed. With speed and skill, the lawyer tied up the loose ends. Bringing Ebenezer Balfour before the courts would almost certainly put Alan at risk. He was also an old man. So it was agreed that he could live out his remaining years in the House of Shaws, but that the bulk of the money from the estate would be mine.

The following day Alan and I left the House of Shaws and set out for Edinburgh. We shook hands and said good-by on the outskirts.

I went on into the city alone to arrange a safe and secret passage to France for Alan Breck Stewart.

But...that is another story.

Stories . . .
that have stood the test of time

Ladybird titles cover a wide range of subjects and reading ages.
Write for a free illustrated list from the publishers:
LADYBIRD BOOKS, INC. Auburn, Maine 04210

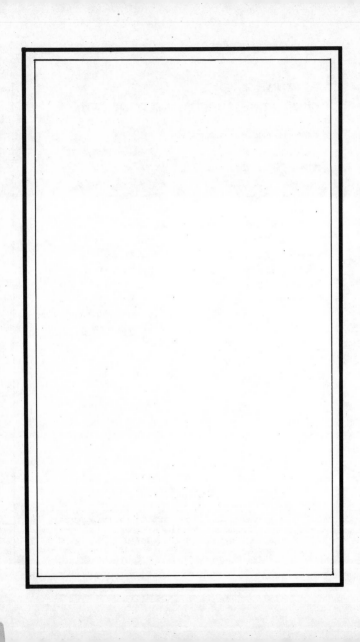